BY JAKE MADDOX

illustrated by Sean Tiffany

text by Lisa Trumbauer

Librarian Reviewer
Chris Kreie
Media Specialist, Eden Prairie Schools, MN
MS in Information Media, St. Cloud State University, MN

Reading Consultant
Mary Evenson
Middle School Teacher, Edina Public Schools, MN
MA in Education, University of Minnesota

Impact Books are published by Stone Arch Books
A Capstone Imprint
151 Good Counsel Drive, P.O. Box 669
Mankato, Minnesota 56002
www.capstonepub.com

Library of Congress Cataloging-in-Publication Data

Maddox, Jake.
    Kart Crash / by Jake Maddox; illustrated by Sean Tiffany.
    p. cm. — (Impact Books. A Jake Maddox Sports Story)
    ISBN 978-1-4342-0777-7 (library binding)
    ISBN 978-1-4342-0873-6 (pbk.)
    [1. Karting—Fiction.] I. Tiffany, Sean, ill. II. Title.
PZ7.M25643Kar 2009
[Fic]—dc22   2008004290

Summary: When Austin moves, he leaves his kart behind. How can he
compete at the new track when he's driving a rental?

Art Director: Heather Kindseth
Graphic Designer: Kay Fraser

Printed in the United States of America in Stevens Point, Wisconsin.
022010
005705R

TABLE OF CONTENTS

CHAPTER 1

NEW TRACK CHALLENGE

What if I crash?

Austin tried to ignore the thought that dashed through his mind. His go-kart hugged the track. Austin sat just inches from the ground. Dark asphalt rushed past. The kart's wide tires gripped the ground.

New racetracks were always a big challenge. The track was new to Austin. A crash wouldn't be unheard of for a new racer at a track.

Austin held on tight to the steering wheel. The curve in the track was coming up. He eased his foot slightly off the gas pedal. The curve didn't look too tight, but Austin didn't want to take any chances.

Some of the other racers on the track were not as careful. Several people flew past. "They know the track better than I do," Austin said to himself. "That's what I get for being the new kid on the track."

Austin pushed down on the gas pedal a little more. His heart beat quickly. His hands were sweating inside his gloves.

He turned the steering wheel to the left. The go-kart coasted along the turn. It never even came close to the bales of hay lined along the track's edge. The hay was there to soften the blow from a crash.

Austin came out of the turn and into the final straightaway. The finish line was only a few hundred yards ahead. About half a dozen karts were between Austin and the end of the race.

He pushed down harder on the gas pedal, and the kart burst forward. He flicked the steering wheel right and left as he moved past one kart, then another, then another. Soon only two karts were between him and the finish line.

Austin was sure he could pass them. He imagined a path between them and gave the go-kart as much gas as possible.

He was almost there. Seconds later, Austin flew past the finish line, but not past the other two drivers. He finished in third place.

Slowing down, Austin pulled off to the side of the track. He lined up with the other racers. He pushed himself up from the go-kart and looked down at it in disgust.

"That's what I get for driving a rental," he mumbled. He had to stop himself from kicking the tires. Instead, he tore off his helmet and scowled.

The second-place driver walked over to him. Austin recognized the blue kart and the driver's matching blue suit from the track. The driver took off his helmet.

Then Austin realized that the driver wasn't a boy. She was a girl. Her long brown hair tumbled from her helmet. "Good race," she said, walking up to Austin.

"If you think placing third is good," Austin said.

"You beat twenty other drivers," she said, smiling. "I'd call that pretty good."

Austin shrugged. "I guess," he admitted.

"You're new here, right?" she asked.

"Yeah. My family just moved from Virginia," Austin answered.

"Well, welcome to Missouri!" the girl said. "My name is Nicole."

"I'm Austin," Austin said.

A crowd of people had gathered around the guy who'd won. They were congratulating him.

"Who's that?" Austin asked Nicole.

"That's Ryan Stone," Nicole said. "And if you want to win at this track, he's the one you have to beat."

THE ONE TO BEAT

Austin studied the boy standing beside the red go-kart. His safety suit matched his kart. It was as if the go-kart and suit were meant to go together.

As Austin watched, Ryan accepted everyone's congratulations. His smile was confident, like he knew he belonged in the winner's circle.

"You must have raced back in Virginia," Nicole said.

"I did," Austin said. "I had my own kart and everything."

"Well, it shows," Nicole told him. "You definitely know what you're doing."

"Yeah," Austin said sadly. "Too bad we had to leave my kart behind. Now I'm stuck with renting one."

"The rentals here at Hammerside Track aren't that bad," Nicole said. "My kart's a rental."

Austin eyed the blue kart parked in front of his own. "I guess it didn't hurt your chances in the race," he said.

Nicole laughed and said, "Well, I didn't win, but I'll take second place. And it's nearly impossible to beat Ryan."

"Why?" Austin asked. "His kart looks cool, but is it really that much better?"

Nicole shrugged. "Maybe. He's also a really good driver. He goes to the kart school in town."

"Go-kart school?" Austin said, frowning. "I don't need a school to teach me how to drive a go-kart. I just need better equipment."

"Come on," Nicole said. "Let me introduce you to Ryan."

Austin didn't want to meet the winner. But he knew that being a good sport was part of racing. It just wasn't a part he liked.

He wished his chances had been better. His own kart back home would have made things way more even.

"Ryan!" Nicole called out.

The red-haired boy turned his head and raised a hand. "Hey, Nicole," he said.

"Ryan, this is Austin," Nicole said, pointing at Austin. "He's a new racer, just moved here from Virginia."

Ryan tucked his helmet under his arm. Austin thought he looked like he was having his picture taken.

"Not a bad race," Ryan said.

"Nice kart," Austin said, nodding toward Ryan's go-kart.

"Thanks," Ryan said. He glanced at Austin's kart. "You've got a nice kart, too. For a rental," he added.

Austin frowned. "I had my own kart back home in Virginia," he told Ryan. "It would have been great at this track."

Ryan smiled and said, "Sure it would have. Why didn't you bring it with you?"

Austin didn't want to go into the reasons for his family's move. "I just couldn't, that's all," he said, shrugging.

"Too bad," Ryan said. "A good kart is important to win on this track."

Nicole laughed. "Lighten up, Ryan!" she said. "You'll scare Austin away. And we need all the good drivers we can get."

Austin frowned. He could fight his own battles. "I don't scare that easily," he said.

"Good," Ryan said. "We'll be facing each other on the track a lot."

Someone called Ryan's name, and Ryan turned and waved. "See you guys," he said. Then he started walking away.

"What was that about needing all the good drivers?" Austin asked Nicole.

"At the end of the month, we have a big relay race," Nicole told him. "Only the best drivers can enter."

"Only the best drivers with the best karts," Austin said, scowling down at his rented go-kart once more.

CHAPTER 3

GO-KART CENTRAL

The next afternoon, Austin stood outside the window of the go-kart store. He looked at the karts on the showroom floor.

One of them, a dark green kart, looked a lot like the kart he'd left behind in Virginia. Austin knew that if he had his old kart, he could have beat Ryan the day before.

A shadow appeared on the window beside him. It was Nicole, the girl Austin had met at the track.

"Still want your own kart?" Nicole asked.

"Sure, who doesn't?" Austin said.

Nicole shrugged. "I don't think it's that important," she said.

Austin looked at her as if she'd grown a second head. "Of course it is!" he exclaimed. "The kart is half the battle. Without a good kart, you can't win."

Nicole shook her head. Then she began to walk away.

"Hey! Where are you going?" Austin called after her.

Nicole turned around. "Do you really want to see what good driving is all about?" she asked. "Then come with me."

Austin looked at the karts in the window one more time. Then he followed Nicole.

She walked around the corner. She headed down an alley between two buildings. For a moment, she disappeared, and Austin had to rush to catch up.

Then he heard it. Go-kart engines.

At the end of the alley there was a door, and through the door was a large practice track. The track seemed to be behind the go-kart shop.

The track was an oval. It had dips and curves, but basically just went around and around. About a dozen karts were whizzing around the track.

"What is this place?" Austin shouted above the motors.

"This is GKC," Nicole replied. "Go-Kart Central. It's the go-kart school I was telling you about."

Austin looked more closely. He noticed a few adults standing around, talking into microphones.

"Those are the instructors," Nicole told him. "They're talking to some of the drivers through special earphones in their helmets."

Austin continued to watch. Suddenly, a red kart rolled onto the track. Austin recognized Ryan's kart right away. He watched as Ryan pulled up to an instructor, nodded, and then took off.

Austin didn't want to stare at Ryan's kart, but he couldn't help it. The kart flew around the track, much more smoothly than the other karts did. It slid through turns and swirled through dips. It dashed between other karts and always came away free.

Ryan's kart was more than a go-kart, Austin realized. It was a perfect machine.

"Ryan comes out here almost every day to practice," Nicole said.

"You can practice," Austin said. "But you still need the right equipment."

One of the adult instructors walked up to them. "Hey, Nicole," the man said. "Are you here for a practice session?"

"Not for me today, Mike," Nicole said. "My friend Austin might be, though. He just moved here from Virginia. He used to race there."

"Virginia has some good kart schools," Mike said. "Which school did you go to?"

Austin smiled. "I didn't have to go to school to learn how to race," he told the instructor. "I picked it up on my own."

"Good for you," Mike said. "If you change your mind, though, come on back. We're always looking for new students. And new talent."

Austin watched the drivers and go-karts for a few more minutes. Then he said, "Well, I better get going."

"See you later," Nicole said.

In front of the go-kart shop, Austin looked in the window a final time. The karts all gleamed.

Austin kicked the ground and turned away. There was another race on Saturday. It would be his second time on the Hammerside track. Now that he was more familiar with the track, he was sure he could come out on top.

Rental or no rental.

CRASH!

CHAPTER 4

Saturday morning was cool and breezy. It was a perfect track day.

In the changing room at the track, Austin put on his green racing suit. Just having it on made him feel better. He felt more in control.

He grabbed his helmet and gloves. He felt happy as he walked outside into the bright sun.

Then he saw his rental kart.

The kart wasn't horrible. It just wasn't his. The color was boring, and the cart had a few scratches. It was pretty clear that it had been around the track a few times.

Austin leaned down and inspected the tires. They were smooth and even, just right for gripping the asphalt of the track.

Feeling a bit more confident, Austin slid down into the kart. He started the engine. He listened to it roar and purr.

Suddenly, Austin felt full of energy. He was ready. He was ready to prove himself on this track. He was ready to show that he could do it. He was a great racer.

He lined up with the other karts on the grid. He was in the middle of the pack, so he'd have to make up some ground if he hoped to get anywhere near the top racers.

Then the green flag went down. They were off. Austin pushed on the gas pedal and sped forward. He broke away from the line of cars. Soon, he was passing karts on his right and his left. Ryan's kart was so close. Only a few karts separated them.

Then Austin saw that Ryan was slowing down for the next curve. "Now I'll pass him!" Austin said to himself.

Instead of easing up on the gas, Austin's foot pushed down. The kart shot forward. It entered the turn at a sharp angle. The back end of the kart swung back and forth. Austin gave the kart more gas, but it was too late.

Austin slid off the track and flew right into a bale of hay.

Smash!

NO ONE TO BLAME

CHAPTER 5

Austin sat, stunned, in his go-kart.

Clumps of hay clung to his shoulders and helmet. Hay covered the front of the kart and hung from the tires. Some hay even stuck out of the mouthpiece of his helmet.

All around him, go-karts whizzed by. His crash hadn't stopped the race for the other drivers, just for him.

Finally, the other karts had all flown past, headed for the finish line. Then Austin knew it was safe to leave his go-kart, and he pulled himself out.

At the same time, two track officials came riding up in a golf cart. "Austin!" one shouted. "Are you okay?"

Austin took off his helmet and nodded. But it wasn't true. Actually, he'd never felt worse. He was sure his face was flaming red, redder than Ryan Stone's car.

Together, Austin and the track officials pushed the go-kart away from the wall of hay. The engine started right away, and Austin coasted the kart back to the main track building.

As he got out of the kart, he couldn't help but notice Ryan standing nearby.

Once again, Ryan was surrounded by fans. Once again, he was accepting the congratulations for a good race.

This time, Austin knew he had no one to blame but himself.

"What happened to you back there?" Nicole asked as she walked over.

Austin shrugged, trying to play it cool. "Just lost control, I guess," he said.

Nicole narrowed her eyes and asked, "You were trying to get ahead of Ryan, weren't you?"

"I was trying to win the race," Austin said. He tried to change the subject. "How did you do?"

"I came in fourth," Nicole said, "but my qualifying time was still pretty good."

"Qualifying time?" Austin asked. "Qualifying for what?"

"For the big relay race at the end of the month," Nicole told him. "They take an average of race times, and the top six racers enter the event as a team."

Austin thought for a minute. Then he asked, "How many races do you need to do to be in the relay race?"

"Five," Nicole said.

"That's just great," Austin said. "I've only had one, and I just wasted this race. And the relay race is only a couple of weeks away."

"You can also make up race times at GKC," Nicole said. "The relay race officials will allow practice times, if you tell them ahead of time."

"I don't know about GKC," Austin said. "The only way to really race is to just do it. You can't get the feel for the track if you're just driving around in circles on a practice lap."

"Maybe not," Nicole said. "But you could probably learn some tricks and stuff. And it will also help you learn more about the other racers."

Austin looked over at Ryan Stone. Nicole had a point. If he went on the practice track with Ryan, he'd learn how to beat this guy.

"Besides," Nicole said. "Maybe the practice track will help you learn how not to crash."

PRACTICE TIME

Austin headed to GKC the next day. As he walked in, Mike, the instructor, smiled at him.

"Hey, Austin!" Mike said, waving. "Nice to see you again!"

"Just thought I'd get in some practice time," Austin said. He tried to sound like it didn't matter, like he didn't really need the practice. "I love to race," he added. "Once a week doesn't seem like enough sometimes."

"That's how a lot of the kids feel around here," Mike said. "Come on. Let me get you set up."

Mike led Austin to a big, barnlike room. The floor was lined with go-karts. They weren't the shiny, brand-new models he'd seen in the store window. All of them were used. Still, Austin's heart sped up at the sight.

Mike smiled. "There's something about racing that just gets into your blood," he said. "There's no other feeling like it."

Austin just nodded.

"Well, pick out a kart, and come on outside," Mike said.

Austin chose one that looked a lot like the go-kart he'd left at home. It was a shiny green kart with twin white stripes.

He stepped into the snug seat and sat down. He put on his helmet and gloves. After twisting the key, he slowly drove the kart forward. He moved it away from the line of cars and toward the large open door.

Austin had no problem figuring out the direction of the track. Groups of people were gathered around it. Engine noises echoed through his helmet.

Mike met Austin at the edge of the track. He handed Austin a small earphone. "Put this in your helmet," he instructed. "I'll call out advice as you drive, okay?"

Austin nodded and slid the earphone into his ear. Racers always wore earplugs on the track to protect their hearing. Even though he was wearing earplugs, Austin could still hear Mike's voice.

He put his hand on the steering wheel and took a deep breath. Then he pushed down on the gas pedal ever so slightly and joined the rest of the drivers on the track.

"Good, Austin!" Mike said through the earphone. "Now keep going, steady. Nothing too big at first."

Austin knew Mike was right. He should take it slow. But the power of the go-kart called to him. He knew it was just a practice run, but it still felt like a race. He wanted to get ahead of one more kart. Then he could dash around one more line. Then he could get around one more curve.

On the earphone, Mike warned Austin a few times, but he didn't pay attention.

And then he saw it. A flash of red and gold. Ryan Stone had driven onto the track.

CHAPTER 7

ONLY CHANCE

"Austin! Slow down!" Mike shouted in Austin's earphone.

Austin heard him, but didn't pay attention. He concentrated on driving.

Austin knew the rules of the practice track. He knew he wasn't supposed to take chances. He was supposed to do what the instructor said.

But he also knew that he had to prove to himself that he was as good as Ryan.

Austin sped up. He rushed past several karts, pulling closer and closer to Ryan. Only two karts were between them. Then only one. Finally, Austin was directly behind Ryan.

Austin turned the steering wheel slightly to the left. He would take the inside of the track, away from the outside wall.

His front tire was almost even with Ryan's back tire. Only inches separated them.

Austin knew if he made one wrong move, his kart would bounce right off Ryan's tire.

He kept his hands steady on the wheel. He moved closer and closer. Now his front tire was past Ryan's back tire. It was nearly to the middle of Ryan's go-kart.

One extra push on the gas pedal, and Austin knew he'd have Ryan beat.

"Austin!" Mike's voice crackled in Austin's ear. "You need to back off. You're too close!"

Austin kept going. He could feel his kart beginning to take the low turn around the oval. He knew the outer edge was slightly steeper and longer. It would take Ryan a split second longer to make the turn.

The split second was all Austin needed to pull in front.

"Come on, come on!" Austin whispered.

The two karts were now even, neck and neck. Their front tires were side by side.

Austin glanced over at Ryan's red helmet. It sparkled in the sunlight.

Ryan's eyes were focused on the track, not on the car next to him. Austin turned the wheel of his kart, and he sped around the shorter inner track. He pulled off ahead of Ryan and tore off down the straightaway.

He knew Ryan was close behind him, but he didn't check the distance. He didn't want to give up any ground. A few slower karts were still working their way around the track. Austin knew he should slow down. He knew it was dangerous to race so fast on the practice track.

But he couldn't slow down. He might never beat Ryan again. This was his chance.

Finally, he sped across the starting point, several kart-lengths ahead of Ryan Stone.

ALL THAT FOR NOTHING

Austin leaped from his kart and slipped off his helmet. He couldn't help the huge smile spreading across his face.

Mike was not smiling when he ran over. "What were you doing out there?" he growled. "This isn't the place to show off. We have beginners out there."

Austin's smile started to fade. Mike was right, of course. He shouldn't have gone that fast. Still, it had felt great.

"I was just testing myself," Austin said.

"And you wanted to see if you could beat me," Ryan said, walking up behind him.

Austin turned. "Yeah. That too," he said.

Austin and Ryan glared at each other. Finally, Ryan spoke. "Practice track is one thing. The racetrack is something else."

"Of course," Austin said. "But if I want to enter that relay race with you, I have to make up some qualifying times. I thought I'd get a jump start today."

"Did you tell that to Mike?" Ryan asked.

"Well, not really," Austin admitted.

"Then this practice run doesn't count anyway," Ryan said, shaking his head. "All that for nothing."

Then Ryan turned and walked away.

Austin sighed. Ryan was right. Another chance wasted.

He turned and looked at Mike. "I'm sorry about that, Mike," he said. "I was just trying to beat the best driver on the track."

Mike shook his head. "Ryan is an excellent driver, but you need to learn how to race with him, not against him," he said.

Austin frowned. "Race with him?" he asked. "I don't get it. Aren't I supposed to beat him?"

"Sure," Mike told him. "But karting isn't just about racing by yourself. And it's more than just knowing your kart. You also have to figure out what the other drivers will do. You have to read their moves and adjust your own."

Then Mike walked away, and Nicole walked over.

"That's pretty good advice, don't you think?" Nicole asked.

Austin said, "When I raced in Virginia, I just jumped in and took off. I didn't think of strategy and stuff. And I usually won. I also had the fastest kart on the track."

"Oh, you and your old kart!" Nicole said, rolling her eyes. "If it was so great, why did you leave it behind?"

Austin straightened his shoulders. He guessed he could tell her. It wasn't a huge secret. He just didn't like talking about it.

"It's no big deal, really," he told Nicole. "We moved out here to be with my grandparents. They didn't have room for the go-kart at their place, so we sold it."

"So get over it, and get back to racing," Nicole said.

Austin knew she was right.

He jammed his helmet back on his head. This time, when he stepped into the driver's seat, he did it with a clear purpose.

He would prove himself, and he'd improve his racing skills.

Austin coasted back onto the track.

THE BIG RACE

After a few weeks, Austin had gotten all of the qualifying times he needed. On the last Saturday of the month, he headed to the track for the big relay race.

Austin lined up with the other drivers on the starting line. His yellow rental kart shook beneath him. He eyed the other drivers around him.

The track was full. More than twenty karts waited for the race to begin.

It was only a heat, but it was Austin's first heat of the day. He just had to do well in the heats in order to make the final race and the championship.

He would race in three heats, and only then would he know if he'd made the finals.

Austin was full of energy. He felt the energy from his kart. He felt the energy from the other drivers on the track.

His heart beat loudly under his suit. The race day was ahead of him. He was really excited.

Finally, it was time for the first heat to begin. Even though Austin had qualified for the race, he was still new to the track. Because of that, he was still considered a beginner.

His position was toward the back of the pack. He had a lot of ground to make up.

The green flag went down, and Austin shot off with the rest of the drivers. He steered and quickly drove past a number of karts.

He came around the first curve in the oval track, passing several karts that had been ahead of him. His goal was to finish in a good position during the first heat.

Austin coasted into the straightaway on the far side of the track. He pulled away from a few other karts. He slid around the next turn, barely feeling the track as it flew beneath his tires.

The first heat was great. Austin cruised into the final lap, feeling good about his driving and his time.

As he got out of his kart at the end of the heat, Nicole ran up to him.

"Awesome race!" she said. She had raced in the heat just before Austin's, along with Ryan.

"It felt good," Austin said. "Now I just have to make sure I keep it up during the next two heats."

Austin checked the list to see who he would be racing with next. Nicole wasn't on the list, but Ryan was.

Austin tried to remember that in this race, he wasn't racing against Ryan. He was racing with him.

Ryan would be his teammate, after all, if Austin made it to the finals. And to make it to finals, he'd have to do well in the last two heats.

Austin strapped his helmet back on and slipped on his gloves. Then he hopped into his go-kart.

The green flag flashed down, and Austin took off. He tried to pay attention to the track in front of him, as well as to all the other karts. Up ahead, Ryan's red kart flashed under the sun. Austin inched forward. He took a few more chances than he should have.

Austin didn't do anything wrong, though. He was careful on the track. He didn't pass anyone dangerously. He moved his kart through the line of racers, giving his kart a little more gas than perhaps he needed to.

Then Ryan lost control of his go-kart. Ryan's kart spun in the sun and smashed into the wall.

ONE MORE HEAT

Austin sped up around the track. He knew he should race past Ryan and get into position to win the heat.

Instead, his foot found the brake pedal. Austin found himself steering toward the wall.

He pulled up behind Ryan's kart. Quickly, he leaped out.

"Hey! Ryan!" Austin said, rushing over. He kept his helmet on. "Are you okay?"

Austin saw Ryan shake his head, as if to clear it. He looked up at Austin through the tinted shield of his helmet.

"What are you doing? Get back to the race!" Ryan yelled.

"I thought you might need some help!" Austin said.

"I'm fine. I just made a stupid move. Keep going!" Ryan replied. "You can still win the heat!"

"No, I can't. It's too late. It doesn't matter now," Austin told him. "I already stopped. I'll just wait with you until the track officials get here."

Austin went back to his own kart. He knew it was safer to stay inside his kart than to stay on the track with other karts speeding by.

Soon the last car passed, and the track officials rode up. They checked out Ryan's kart.

Then Austin and Ryan both eased away from the wall and drove their karts back around the track. Then they parked and got out.

"Are you guys all right?" Nicole said, running up.

"Sure," Ryan said. He turned to Austin. "You shouldn't have stopped, you know. You were our best chance of getting ahead in the finals."

Austin shrugged. "I think we can still both make it to the finals. We still have one heat to go, don't we?" he asked. "We still have a chance."

"That's right, we do!" Ryan said.

"Yeah, you do," Nicole said. "Your times in the first heat were really good. So if I were you, I'd get back in your karts and get back out there."

"What do you say?" Ryan asked Austin.

"Absolutely!" Austin said. "I just hope the wreck didn't hurt your kart too much. Do you think it's okay?"

"This thing?" Ryan said, pointing at his kart. "It's fine. Besides, that's what's so good about a rental. You can always turn it in for something else."

Austin's mouth fell open. "A rental? Are you serious?" he said.

Ryan laughed and said, "What, you thought this thing was mine? No way. My parents can't afford a kart. This kart is a rental."

"Why'd you make all those comments about my rental, then?" Austin asked.

"I wanted you to get nervous," Ryan said. "I didn't want you to know we were even. Then you wouldn't have tried so hard to beat me. And I wouldn't have tried so hard to stay ahead."

Now it was Austin's turn to laugh. "Well, it sure worked. You really fooled me!" he said.

Ryan threw his arm around Austin's shoulder. "Come on," he said. "Let's ace this next heat, and I'll see you in the finals."

"And this time, my rental will beat your rental," Austin said.

"It just might," Ryan said. "After all, it's not about the kart."

"That's right. It's all about the driver," Austin said.

The call went up for the next heat, and Austin and Ryan headed over to find their place in line.

ABOUT THE AUTHOR

Lisa Trumbauer is the *New York Times* best-selling author of *A Practical Guide to Dragons*. In addition, she has written about 300 other books for children, including mystery novels, picture books, and nonfiction books on just about every topic under the sun (including the sun!). Lisa lives in New Jersey with her husband, Dave, two moody cats, and a dog named Blue.

ABOUT THE ILLUSTRATOR

When Sean Tiffany was growing up, he lived on a small island off the coast of Maine. Every day, from sixth grade until he graduated from high school, he had to take a boat to get to school. When Sean isn't working on his art, he works on a multimedia project called "OilCan Drive," which combines music and art. He has a pet cactus named Jim.

GLOSSARY

asphalt (ASS-fawlt)—a black, tarlike substance that is mixed with sand and gravel and then rolled flat to make roads

coasted (KOHST-id)—moved a vehicle without using any power

confident (KON-fuh-duhnt)—having a strong belief in your own abilities; certain that things will happen the way you want

earphone (EER-fohn)—a small speaker that is placed inside the ear, on which the listener can hear music or other sounds

heat (HEET)—a trial run in a race

qualifying (KWAL-uh-fye-ing)—a race time that is fast enough to permit the racer to advance to the next level

relay (REE-lay)—a race with several members on a team

rent (RENT)—to give or get something in exchange for payment

rental (RENT-uhl)—something that is rented

straightaway (STRAYT-uh-way)—a stretch of racetrack that is not curved

MORE ABOUT

Go-karts can be really expensive. Mini karts for little kids can cost $700, and full-size karts can be as much as $4,000!

Most kids don't have their own go-karts. Some racetracks and kart schools rent go-karts to kids who don't have their own karts. Usually, karts are rented by the hour or for one race at a time.

If you have your own go-kart, you need to take good care of it. It's almost like having a real car! You'll need to make sure to maintain your kart so that it keeps you racing fast — and safely — for as long as possible.

There are go-kart schools and racetracks all over the country. To find one near you, use the Internet to search or look through the phone book.

GO-KARTS

It's possible to build your own go-kart. You would need to start by finding a book on building go-karts. The next step would be to find all of the parts and tools needed to complete the kart. You should ask a teacher, coach, parent, or other adult friend to help you as you build your go-kart.

Safety is always important, but it's especially important when you're zooming around the racetrack! Before you ever start the engine, you need to know how to start, stop, speed up, and slow down your kart. You must wear a helmet at all times. You shouldn't drive faster than the limit at your track or school. And you need to make sure to watch out for other drivers — for your safety and for theirs!

HAVE FUN!

DISCUSSION QUESTIONS

1. How does Austin feel after his first
   go-kart race at the new track? Why?

2. Have you ever moved to a new city or
   new school? What are some good things
   about moving? What are some of the
   bad things?

3. What do you think will happen to Ryan
   and Austin at the end of the race day
   that begins in the final chapter?

WRITING PROMPTS

1. Write a letter from Austin to a friend back home in Virginia. Write about Austin's experiences at the Hammerside track.

2. Austin loves to race go-karts. Write an essay from Austin's point of view that explains why he enjoys karting. Then write a paragraph from your point of view. Do you think you'd like to race go-karts? Why or why not?

3. Imagine that Austin is telling younger drivers about racing. What might Austin tell them? Write a few paragraphs that tell Austin's karting instructions and advice.

OTHER BOOKS

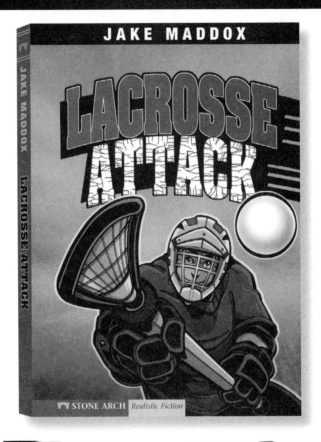

Peter made the varsity lacrosse team. But the team's captain doesn't want Peter to take his position. He'll stop at nothing to make Peter quit. Will Peter give up, or can he prove he deserves to be on the team?

BY JAKE MADDOX

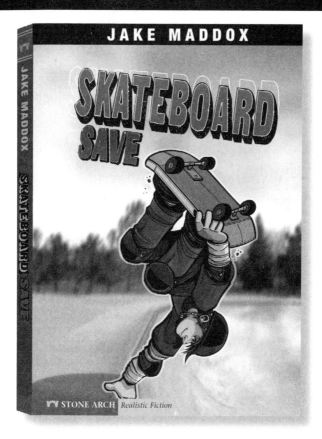

The biggest skating contest of the year is coming up. When Bernie's board breaks during the final round of the contest, will Riley help him, or will he use the accident to win?

INTERNET SITES

Do you want to know more about subjects related to this book? Or are you interested in learning about other topics? Then check out FactHound, a fun, easy way to find Internet sites.

Our investigative staff has already sniffed out great sites for you!

Here's how to use FactHound:

1. Visit *www.facthound.com*

2. Select your grade level.

3. To learn more about subjects related to this book, type in the book's ISBN number: **9781434207777**.

4. Click the **Fetch It** button.

FactHound will fetch the best Internet sites for you!